Mabee and the Gravy

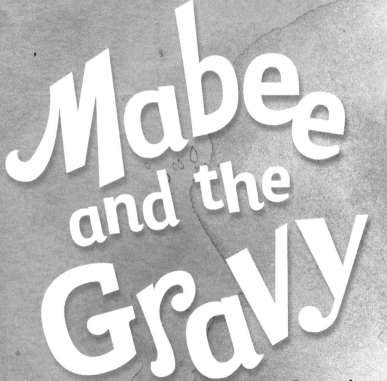

Mabee and the Gravy

Story by
Allen Edgar Rogers

Illustrations by
Whitney Hill

BELLE ISLE BOOKS
www.belleislebooks.com

ISBN: 978-1-953021-13-7
LCCN: 2021914329

Printed in the United States of America

Published by
Belle Isle Books (an imprint of Brandylane Publishers, Inc.)
5 S. 1st Street
Richmond, Virginia 23219

BELLE ISLE BOOKS
www.belleislebooks.com

belleislebooks.com | brandylanepublishers.com

**To Colleen
and our dads**

Mabee did not like flowers

or taking hot showers

or being forced to read
schoolbooks for hours.

She didn't like babies

or little old ladies—

and Mabee most certainly

did not like gravy.

"I don't know what's in it,
but I know I won't like it,"
cried Mabee, sounding quite
a bit childish.

YUMMMMM!

"But Mabee, it's gravy!"
her mother exclaimed.
"It's delicious and filling,
and what a fun name!

It's exciting, you know,
to try something new.
You never know what you will find
till you do."

"I don't like things
I don't already know,"

Mabee said as she stomped,
making a show.

I DON'T LIKE NEW THINGS

Her mother first sighed,
then stifled a laugh.
"All right," she said,
"then it's time for your bath."

**"I don't like baths—
the water's too hot!**
And the shampoo we use
puts my hair in a knot."

"I don't like zoos or zoo animals, either—
not hippos, koalas, zebras, or beavers."

"I don't like parks or flowers or babies,
and most of all,
I DO NOT LIKE GRAVY!"

"What do you like, Mabee?
What do you like best?"

"I like what I know,
and I don't like the rest!"

"Is that all?" Mother asked.
"You are missing a lot."
In a huff and a puff,
Mabee scoffed,

"NO I'M NOT!"

The very next day,
Mabee went off to school.
There was a new girl in class
who seemed really cool.

But Mabee remembered,
*I do not like new things,
I won't talk to this new girl
when the bell rings.*

Class was dismissed, and they climbed on the bus.
Students circled the new girl in a loud, joyful fuss.

"Where are you from?" "What brings you here?"

"I wish my mom would let me pierce my ears!"

Mabee was anxious, frustrated, and mad.
Who cares about this new girl?
She's probably BAD!
Mabee considered the trouble this girl'd be.
More friends for her
means less friends for me.

**But then, up she walked—
the new girl, alone.**
She extended a hand
and said softly, "Hello."

"I'm Shirley," she said.
"I like your yellow dress.
It's the best dress I've seen
since I've been here, I'd guess."

LAST WEEK

Mabee blushed—
and, barely able to speak,
said, "Why, thank you.
My mother bought it last week."

"Well, your mom must be cool
and have excellent taste."
"Taste?" Mabee asked.
A smile grew on her face.

"You find your own taste
when you try new things out.
**That's how you discover
what the world's all about.**"

"If you see something new,
give it a try."

Hmm, Mabee thought.

Maybe so. Why don't I?

Mabee and Shirley
became very best friends.
They went on grand adventures,
both real and pretend.

They shared books, art, and music;
they saw some great shows.
They always asked locals,
"Where's the best place to go?"

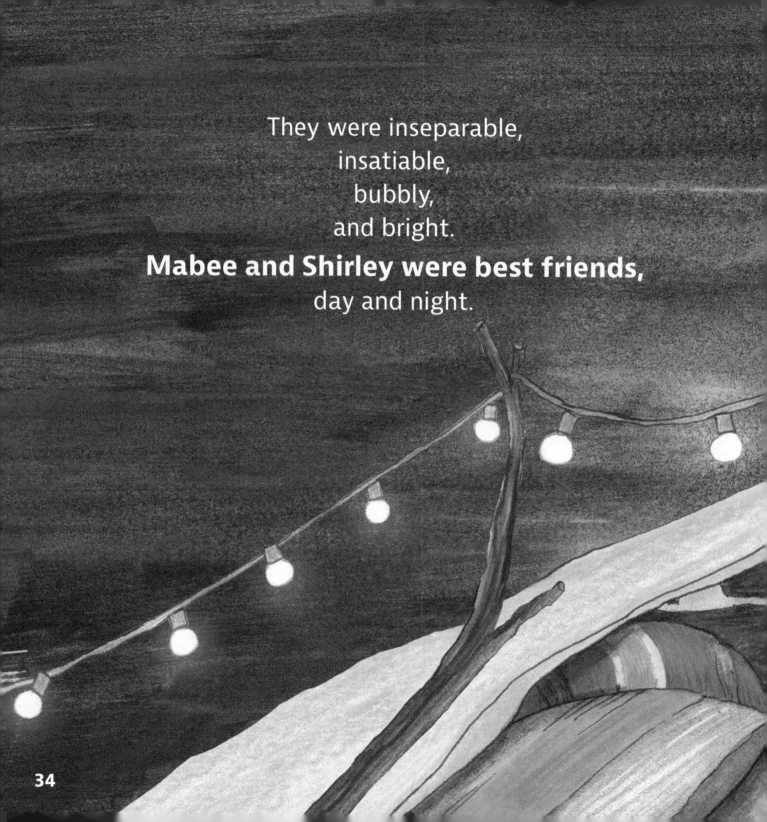

They were inseparable,
insatiable,
bubbly,
and bright.
Mabee and Shirley were best friends,
day and night.

35

But then, one day,
Shirley had to move again.
When Mabee found out,
it made her head spin.

"You can't leave me now!
Please don't go away!
You're my very best friend!
Ask your parents to stay."

"Mabee, we will always be
very best friends,
whether miles apart
or just 'round the bend."

"We'll write every day;

"But, Mabee, we don't know what tomorrow will bring."

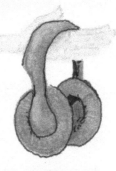

we won't miss a thing!"

"Yes, we will write,
and yes, we will talk,
but at the end of the day,
we will walk our own walk.

We'll discover much more
than we've ever imagined.
Think of all we will do.
Think of all that can happen!"

Mabee did not like this answer,
but she understood.
Shirley had taught her that
change can be good.
It's not always easy;
it's not always fun.
But sometimes it's simply
what has to be done.

So Mabee and Shirley said their goodbyes—
they hugged, and they cried,
and they wiped their wet eyes.

They smiled and waved,
and Shirley drove away.

**For both, tomorrow
would be a new day.**

About the Author

Allen Edgar Rogers is a writer and entrepreneur from southeast Texas. During his career, he has worked in the education, nonprofit, and tech sectors. The common goal of his efforts is to inspire positive change in people and systems. He currently lives in Richmond, Virginia, with his wife, two daughters, and a rescue hound named Gus.

About the Illustrator

Whitney Hill is a creative director and illustrator based in Dallas, Texas. She shares a home with her husband, son, and their dog, Karma. When she's not making art or chasing her son around the backyard, Whitney is pickling vegetables in her kitchen at home—usually green beans.

CPSIA information can be obtained
at www.ICGtesting.com
Printed in the USA
BVHW022347080222
628392BV00009B/334